ARNOLD'S
BURROW

THE PARTY
PLACE

LIZZ'S
LOG

COCO'S
CANOPY

To Helen, Chris,
Katie, and Olivia,
thank you for
everything!

First US edition 2020
First published by Templar Books,
an imprint of Bonnier Books UK 2019

Library of Congress Catalog Card Number pending
ISBN 978-1-5362-1547-2

20 21 22 23 24 25 TLF 10 9 8 7 6 5 4 3

Printed in Dongguan, Guangdong, China

This book was typeset in Trocchi.
The illustrations were done in gouache,
colored pencil, and digital paint.

TEMPLAR BOOKS
an imprint of
Candlewick Press
99 Dover Street
Somerville, Massachusetts 02144

www.candlewick.com

Slow
Samson

Bethany Christou

templar books
an imprint of Candlewick Press

The thing that Samson the sloth
loved more than anything in the world
was to make others happy.

Samson had lots of friends
and got invited to lots of parties,
but there was one problem . . .

HAPPY BIRTHDAY, TERRY!

the party
was starting.

While Samson stopped to sort out an argument . . .

his friends danced the conga.

And while he helped a toppled tortoise . . .

Take care!

his friends sang "Happy Birthday."

By the time Samson finally
arrived, the cake was all gone
and the party had finished.

HAPPY BIRTHDAY, TERRY!

He had missed everything!

Oh no! thought Samson.

It's because I got distracted along the way.

Next time I'm going to **hurry.**

On his way to the next party, Samson didn't stop for the tree frog.

Sorry, got to rush.

Work it out yourselves.

He had no time for the monkeys.

And he charged past the tortoise.

Can't stop!

And if anyone asked for help,
Samson said . . .

He was out of breath
when he arrived . . .

but even at top speed he was
still slow.

He'd been horrible and rude to everyone for nothing!

Without Samson stopping to help, everything had gone wrong.

The tortoise had spent the
whole day stuck on his back.

The tree frog had
no one to talk to.

And the monkeys' arguing had annoyed the whole rain forest.

"I'm just so slow," Samson sobbed.

"No matter what I do, I'll never
make it to a party on time."

Samson's friends were worried about him.

"We need a plan!" said Mac.

Ideas

Together they came up with
lots of different ideas . . .

and one seemed
like it might just work.

The next day, Samson
received a new invitation.

He knew he would be late again, but his
friends were looking forward to seeing him.

He couldn't let them down.

To Samson,
There's a
Party
tomorrow.
usual place,
2 o'clock
Hope you can
make it.
-Mac

Samson set off for the party. This time he didn't hurry.

He stopped to chat
with the tree frog.

Hey,
Fran.

Not
now...

Gotta
dash!

And he was ready to
help the monkeys...

Gotta
go!

and the tortoise.

Can't
stop now...

But they all rushed off when they saw him.
They must be very mad at me, thought Samson.

Samson felt
awfully lonely.

And he was
still slow.

By the time Samson arrived,
he was surc he was hours late.

But to his surprise he found . . .

we ♥

the party had only just begun!

Surprise!

There was dancing,
there were party games,

and there was **plenty** of cake!

But best of all . . .

Best day!

Samson had an amazing time with his friends!

SAMSON
Thanks for drawing us!

So funny!

♥ my friends

BFFs

Everyone agreed that it was the best party yet,
because Samson had been there to share it with them.

Pin the tail

New fri